Pony Tails

WITHDRAWN

May
Takes the Lead

BONNIE BRYANT

Illustrated by Marcy Ramsey

A SKYLARK BOOK
NEW YORK • TORONTO • LONDON • SYDNEY • AUCKLAND

RL5, 009–012
MAY TAKES THE LEAD
A Skylark Book / January 1996

Skylark Books is a registered trademark of Bantam Books,
a division of Bantam Doubleday Dell Publishing Group, Inc.
Registered in U.S. Patent and Trademark Office and elsewhere.
Pony Tails is a trademark of Bonnie Bryant Hiller.

ISBN 0-553-48360-9

Published simultaneously in the United States and Canada

Bantam Books are published by Bantam Books, a division of Bantam
Doubleday Dell Publishing Group, Inc. Its trademark, consisting of the
words "Bantam Books" and the portrayal of a rooster, is Registered in
U.S. Patent and Trademark Office and in other countries. Marca
Registrada. Bantam Books, 1540 Broadway, New York, New York
10036.

PRINTED IN THE UNITED STATES OF AMERICA

OPM   0 9 8 7 6 5 4 3 2 1

For Penny and in memory of Molly
and, of course, Mesa Verde

May
Takes the Lead

1 A Good Cleaning

"I think I need sunglasses!" May Grover said to her pony, Macaroni. "Your golden yellow coat is so sparkly clean, the shine is blinding me!"

Macaroni looked over his shoulder and blinked his eyes slowly. That made May giggle. Maybe his coat was gleaming too brightly for him, too! Then Macaroni turned his attention back to the pile of fresh hay in front of him. He took a bite and munched happily.

May hugged her pony. "I can't let you roll around in the muddy paddock when I'm done with this cleaning," she told him.

May Takes the Lead

"I'm going to cover you with a blanket and keep you in the stall. I won't even give you a chance to be naughty!"

Macaroni gave a little snort.

"Now, now, behave yourself," May teased. Macaroni went back to munching.

May always had fun when she was with Macaroni, even when it seemed to be work. May was working especially hard today to groom Macaroni. She and her best friends, Jasmine James and Corey Takamura, were going to be in a riding demonstration soon. Their Pony Club was helping to raise money for the local County Animal Rescue League, which everybody called CARL because of its initials. It was important for Macaroni to look his very best. People would be paying money to watch him perform.

May, Jasmine, and Corey all lived next door to one another. They had a lot in common. They all had ponies that they kept in their backyards, they all went to the same school, and they were all in the third grade. They also belonged to the same Pony Club, called Horse Wise. Best of all, they were all completely pony crazy. That was why they called themselves the Pony Tails.

Sometimes it seemed as if ponies and horses were May's whole life. Her father was a trainer. That meant he spent most of his time teaching horses for their owners. Mr. Grover loved horses as much as May did. He had a horse named Rascal. May's mother liked to ride as well. She had a bay gelding named Dobbin.

May's two older sisters, Ellie and Dottie, were the only members of the family who didn't have horses. When they were younger, they rode the Grovers' other horse, an old gray named Hank. Now Ellie and Dottie didn't ride anymore. The only thing Ellie cared about was soccer. Dottie was too interested in boys to think about anything else. Sometimes May couldn't believe they were really her sisters!

"Now, let me get the rag and give you a rubdown," May said to Macaroni. "That's the part that *really* makes your coat shine."

Macaroni stood completely still. May could have sworn he was smiling. If he'd

May Takes the Lead

been a cat, he would have been purring! May picked up the rag and began the final touch of her grooming job. It was her favorite part, too.

The phone in the stable rang once, then stopped. May frowned at it. Usually when the phone rang once and stopped, it was May's mother saying she should come into the house because dinner was ready. It wasn't dinnertime yet.

May began rubbing Macaroni on his left shoulder and worked her way back and down, leaving behind a gleaming coat.

The phone rang once again. May looked at the clock by the phone. It still wasn't dinnertime.

"It must be a wrong number," she told Macaroni. He didn't seem to care. He stood still and waited for her to continue rubbing his coat. So she did.

In a few minutes, the phone rang a third time. This time May decided to answer it so she could tell the person who was calling that they were making a mistake. She picked up the phone.

"That's funny," she told Macaroni. "Nobody's there."

Macaroni watched her hang up the phone, waiting for her to return to her important job—making him feel good and clean. May went back to work.

She had finished his left side and was walking around to the right when she heard her sister Dottie call her name.

"May!"

"I'm out here," May answered.

"*May!*" Ellie called.

"In the stable!" May called back.

"*May!*" her sisters yelled together.

May put down the cleaning rag and walked to the door of the stable. Her sisters were standing together at the back door of the house.

"I'm grooming Macaroni!" May said.

"Well, you're supposed to be in here!" said Dottie.

"Didn't you hear the telephone?" Ellie demanded.

"Is dinner ready?" May asked. She was confused.

"Not dinner!" Dottie said.

"The basement!" said Ellie. "Did you forget the deal we made?"

May Takes the Lead

May groaned. She'd forgotten completely. She and her sisters had made a pact with their parents to clean the basement. The Grovers' house had a finished basement that had been a playroom when the girls were little. On rainy days they used to ride bikes down there, make gigantic buildings from blocks, or play with dolls. Even though no one played with those things anymore, they were still there. So were dozens of cartons of old clothes, toys, and papers. Last week Mr. and Mrs. Grover had told the girls that if they cleaned it up they could use it and even have parties in it.

Ellie wanted to invite her soccer team over after practice. Dottie wanted to have a boy-girl party there. May thought it would be fun for the Pony Tails to meet there when the weather kept them out of the hayloft in the stable.

Today was the day the sisters had agreed to do the cleanup.

"I'll be right there," May promised her sisters.

She ducked back into the stable and put

everything into her grooming bucket. She told Macaroni she'd finish the job soon. He didn't look happy when she locked him in his stall.

"I'll be back tomorrow," she promised the pony.

In the basement Ellie handed May a broom. "Didn't you hear the phone ring?" she asked.

"Yes, but I was grooming Macaroni and I—" May started.

"Ponies, ponies. Everything's ponies!" Dottie interrupted. "Some things *are* more important." She pointed to the corner of the basement May was to sweep.

"It's just that grooming—" May tried again.

"*Brooming* is what you're doing today. Not grooming," said Ellie.

Dottie and Ellie wouldn't listen to May. They didn't care about anything that had to do with ponies.

There's no point in trying to explain, May decided. She started sweeping five years' worth of dust and grime from the basement floor. As she worked, she thought about her friends Jasmine and Corey, who were only children and had no sisters.

"You missed a spot!" Ellie pointed out.

My friends are lucky, May decided. *Really* lucky.

2 The Trouble with Sisters

Cleaning the basement wasn't easy work. It especially wasn't easy when May's sisters kept picking on her.

"Don't forget, we're all going to be able to use this room when it's clean," Ellie said.

"We can each have a party in it, but mine will come first because I'm the oldest," said Dottie.

"Then me," Ellie said. "And then, maybe it'll be May's turn."

May knew her sisters were just teasing her. Experience had taught her the best way to respond to that was not to respond at all.

May Takes the Lead

But keeping quiet was not something May did well. After a short time, she couldn't stand her sisters' remarks any longer.

"My birthday comes first," she burst out. "I should have the first party."

"Your birthday?" Dottie looked surprised. "Is it coming up?"

"It's just two weeks away," said May. "And I think I should have a party."

"Since you like ponies so much, why don't you have your birthday party in the stable?" Ellie said.

Dottie seemed to find that very funny. The two of them giggled together.

May didn't giggle at all. She stopped sweeping for a minute and looked at her sisters. "I know you think it's funny, but you guys are really missing out on something by not riding."

"Like what?" Ellie rolled her eyes. "Saddle sores?"

"No—like fun," said May.

"Like I really have time to play with ponies," said Dottie. Dottie was in high school and spent a lot of time on her homework. The rest of her time seemed to be spent on the phone with her boyfriend, Richard.

"It isn't just playing," May said. "We work hard, too. Like right now, we're working on a drill."

"A drill?" Ellie echoed. "What does a power tool have to do with ponies?"

"It's not a power tool—" May began.

"Okay, then, a hand tool. Why would you use a hand tool when a power tool is so much easier?" Dottie asked.

"Not that kind of drill," May said. "It's like—"

"I get it. She's talking about the dentist!" Ellie slapped her hand against her cheek as if she had a bad toothache.

"You know that's not what I mean," May insisted.

"May!" Dottie exclaimed. "If it's not what you mean, why don't you just tell us what you mean?"

May glared at her sisters. Both of them were smirking. They knew what she was talking about. They had both been in Pony Club. Ellie had even been on a drill team.

May Takes the Lead

May tried to swallow her anger. "It's a drill team exercise," she began again. "We're doing it to raise money—"

"Why would they want to drill teeth to raise money?" Ellie interrupted.

"It's what dentists do," said Dottie. "They make lots of money doing it, too."

"I didn't know May was a dentist," said Ellie.

"Must be from looking gift horses in the mouth," Dottie cracked.

Ellie started laughing uncontrollably. Pretty soon, Dottie was laughing, too.

By now May was furious. She wanted to throw down the broom and run out of the basement. But that would have given her sisters too much satisfaction. Instead, she stomped back to the corner where she'd been cleaning. As she swept up the dust, she kept her back to Ellie and Dottie. She didn't pay attention when they started talking about drilling for oil. Or drilling Macaroni's cavities.

Then May couldn't sweep anymore. A stack of cartons was in her way. She put down her broom and looked at a carton.

Pony Tails

On the top it said DOTTIE'S ROOM/PRIVATE!!! Dottie had redecorated her room a few months ago, May remembered. Dottie must have forgotten about this carton after the room was repainted.

May lifted the carton and hauled it over to another part of the room. As she dropped the carton on the floor, the flaps flew open. May glanced over her shoulder. She didn't want Dottie to think she was snooping around her personal stuff.

But Dottie wasn't looking in May's direction. She and Ellie were still talking about drill bits and laughing very hard.

May turned back to the box. On the top of the things inside was a leather-bound book with gold lettering on the cover. It read MY DIARY.

May's eyes widened. She didn't know Dottie kept a diary. What does she write about? May wondered. It seemed like such an interesting thing to do.

May looked at her sisters again. Dottie and Ellie were practically falling on top of one another. They were laughing at some other joke they'd made about drills.

May Takes the Lead

That did it for May. Her sisters didn't care one bit about her feelings. Why should she care about theirs?

Without another thought, she slipped the diary out of the carton and wrapped it in her sweatshirt. Dottie would never notice it was gone, especially if May put the whole carton in a dark corner.

That's just what she did.

3 Backyard Practice

"Good morning, Dobbin. Hello, Rascal. Good boy, Hank," May said, greeting each horse cheerfully as she entered the stable the next morning. "Hi, Macaroni. Now it's time to finish your grooming—as soon as I feed you."

May waved to her father, who was already working in the ring with one of his students, Double-O-Seven. Then she turned her attention to her daily stable chores and taking care of Macaroni. She fed her pony and mucked out his stall. Next she picked up the rag to complete the grooming she'd started the day before.

May Takes the Lead

The back door of May's house slammed. May looked out. There were Jasmine and Corey walking across the lawn. She smiled and waved to her friends. "Ready to go for a ride?" she yelled.

"You bet!" Corey said eagerly. "I'll go get Samurai tacked up."

"Race you!" Jasmine cried. She dashed off to the little stable in her backyard to get her pony ready for a ride.

May hummed to herself as she put on Macaroni's tack. There was nothing she liked to do better than ride with her friends in the Pony Tails. The girls' ponies seemed to enjoy being together, too.

Jasmine's pony was named Outlaw. He was a chestnut with a white face that looked like an outlaw's mask. The mask wasn't the only thing about Jasmine's pony that made him an outlaw. He could be very naughty sometimes, too!

Corey's pony was named Samurai. She called him Sam for short. Sam had a crescent-shaped blaze on his face that looked like a Samurai sword. Most of the time, Sam was a very good pony. But sometimes he would get upset about something, and he would misbehave.

By the time May had finished tacking up Macaroni, her friends were leading their ponies toward the ring behind the Grovers' stable.

Mr. Grover was riding Double-O-Seven at one end of the ring. The girls knew they shouldn't interfere with Double-O-Seven's training, so they stayed at the other end of the ring.

They began by walking in circles to give their ponies a chance to warm up.

"Let's play Follow the Leader," Jasmine suggested when the ponies were all ready to ride. The other Pony Tails agreed that that would be fun. Besides, it would give them a chance to practice the skills they were using at Horse Wise.

"May, you have to be the leader," Corey said.

"Please, May," Jasmine added. "You have such a great imagination. You always think of fun things to do."

"Okay," May agreed cheerfully.

First May led her friends through a snakelike path all around the ring. The

May Takes the Lead

riders had to concentrate to follow exactly where May went. Next May did more snakelike riding, but this time she did it at a trot. Jasmine almost got confused and lost track of the trail, but she followed the pony hoofprints in the ring.

"Now canter!" May called out behind her. She began riding in a large circle. That was easy for her friends to follow and fun, too. All three girls loved to canter on their ponies.

"Now walk again," May said. All three horses began walking.

May slipped her feet out of her stirrups. Corey and Jasmine did the same thing. Corey noticed that when she didn't use her stirrups, she had to pay more attention to her balance.

May put her feet back in the stirrups. She kept on walking Macaroni, but now she took her left hand and put it on top of her head. Corey and Jasmine did the same thing. May kept Macaroni going in circles.

"Hey," Jasmine called, "it's tricky to get Outlaw to turn when I'm holding the reins with only one hand!"

"No kidding," Corey agreed. "Sam's a

little confused about what's going on. But he's paying attention to my leg signals."

"Try this!" said May. She put down her reins and held her arms out to the side. That meant the only way she could tell Macaroni which way to turn was by using her legs. She put pressure on his right side with her whole leg. He hesitated for a few seconds, but then he did it! He turned to the left.

"Good boy!" May said. She turned to look at her friends. They had figured out the same thing, and so had their ponies.

"This is good practice," Corey announced.

"You girls are learning a lot," said Mr. Grover. He was sitting on Double-O-Seven, watching them. "Good job."

"Thanks, Dad." May was practically blushing; she was so pleased by her father's praise. At least someone in the family took her riding seriously!

A few minutes later, the girls stopped their game. They rode in circles together, changing gaits every once in a while.

"I wish *everyone* in my family had nice things to say about my riding," May said.

"What do you mean?" Corey asked.

May told them about the teasing she'd gotten from her sisters the day before. "You two don't know how lucky you are that you don't have older sisters," she added.

Corey and Jasmine looked at each other.

"I don't know about that," Corey said. "Remember the time Ellie let you wear her new sweater?"

"And when Dottie showed us all how to put on lipstick?" Jasmine said.

"Big deal," May said. "Most of the time they don't care about me and Macaroni at all. Right now all they can think about is the parties *they're* going to have in the basement. They don't even care that my birthday is coming up soon."

"Maybe they do care," Corey began. "Maybe—"

Jasmine glanced at Corey. "We'll help you think of something to do for your birthday, May," Jasmine said quickly. "We can talk about it later. We'd better keep riding now. The demonstration for CARL is coming up soon. I want to be ready."

The girls practiced their skills for another fifteen minutes. Then it was time to stop. They walked their ponies in circles to cool them down and talked some more.

"Mom says that only a few people have bought tickets for the show we're putting on," said Corey.

Corey's mother, Dr. Takamura, was a veterinarian whom most people called "Doc Tock." She did some work for CARL, so she knew a lot about the animal shelter.

"Oh, no!" Jasmine said. "We have to make a lot of money for CARL. If only a few people come to our show, the shelter won't have enough money to stay open."

Corey nodded. "Mom says CARL really needs the money. There are a lot of animals who don't have homes or owners to love them. A few of them need special care, too. Medicine for animals can be really expensive."

Jasmine sighed. "I wish I could think of

a way to get more people to buy tickets," she said. "There's got to be something the Pony Tails can do."

Suddenly both girls looked at May.

"Come on, May," Corey said. "You've always got good ideas."

"What?" May hadn't been paying attention to her friends' conversation. She was still thinking about her sisters and the way they'd treated her the day before.

"We need to find a way to tell people about the show for CARL," Jasmine explained. She knew she sounded impatient, but she couldn't help it. How could May be daydreaming when they were talking about something as important as saving animals?

"Oh." May was quiet for a minute. "I can't think of anything," she said.

"You can't?" Corey was amazed. May could always come up with an idea—even if it was a crazy idea.

"I guess my mind is on something else right now," May said.

"Your birthday party?" Corey asked.

"No." May shook her head. "Revenge. Against both my sisters."

May Takes the Lead

Corey and Jasmine didn't like the sound of this.

"Revenge isn't usually a good idea," Jasmine began gently.

"Right," agreed Corey. "Sometimes it can get you into big trouble. Remember?"

May remembered. Not too long ago, she'd tried to get back at Wil McNally. He was a bully who had been picking on Jasmine. Her plan had backfired, and Jasmine had wound up angry at May.

"This is different, though," May insisted. "That time I was trying to solve Jasmine's problem. This time it's *my* problem. I get to decide how to fix it."

Corey and Jasmine looked at one another. They were about to warn May again when they heard the phone in the stable ring once.

"That must be Ellie and Dottie calling me back to work," May announced. "I don't want to keep them waiting today." May dismounted and walked Macaroni back toward the stable. "See you," she said, waving good-bye to her friends.

Corey and Jasmine walked their ponies

back out of the schooling ring and rode toward their own stables.

"What are we going to do about this?" Corey asked Jasmine.

"I don't know," Jasmine answered. "But when May gets an idea in her head . . ."

"It usually stays there," Corey finished Jasmine's thought.

The girls reached Corey's stable. "See you tomorrow," Corey called.

"Bye," Jasmine called back.

Corey had a lot of work to do grooming and feeding Samurai. It gave her time to think about May and her sisters. If only May knew . . .

4 Temptation

The rest of the day was very busy for May. She thought about her plan to get back at her sisters, but she didn't have time to do anything about it. After she finished helping Ellie and Dottie in the basement, she had to return to the stable to groom and feed Macaroni. Then it was time for dinner, and time to set the table. When the meal was over she had to help her mother clean up.

Finally May shoved the last pot into the cabinet and hurried to her room. Quickly she closed the door behind her. She was alone at last!

Pony Tails

May got on her hands and knees and reached under her bed. She felt for the big box filled with clothes that didn't fit Ellie anymore but didn't fit May yet. May pulled the box toward her.

There, on the top, was the sweatshirt she'd been wearing yesterday. Carefully she took it out of the box and unfolded it.

Resting inside was the leather-bound diary.

May looked at the book. It had a flap of leather that came from the back and latched on the front. There was a lock on the latch. May didn't have the key. She didn't even know where the key was. It was probably in Dottie's room, but maybe Dottie kept it on a string around her neck. If May had a diary, that's what she'd do with the key. She would never want to worry about who might find the key and decide to open *her* diary.

The lock on this diary wasn't a very sturdy one. May could probably force it open. Even if she couldn't unlock it, she could always just cut the leather strap with scissors.

Pony Tails

MY DIARY.

The gold words seemed to gleam up at her, bright and inviting.

May felt the smooth, soft cover with her hands. She sniffed at it. It had the same nice smell as clean tack. It was real leather.

May knew it wasn't right to read someone else's diary, but so what? Dottie hadn't thought twice about teasing May yesterday. And tonight at dinner, she'd gone on and on about how she was having friends over first—on Saturday night.

May touched the latch, feeling the cool metal lock. It would be so interesting to find out Dottie's most private thoughts. Maybe she had written about her boyfriends. And about school . . .

"School," May said out loud. "Oh no. I have math homework to do!"

May ran her fingers over the soft leather cover of the diary one more time. Then she wrapped it back in the sweatshirt and slid the box under her bed.

Operation Get Back at Dottie and Ellie will have to wait, May told herself. Right now she had to write out the eights tables.

5 A Good Idea

"Look at him! He's my favorite. He's so cute!" Corey said, pointing to a newborn puppy with a little fuzz of white fur on his sweet, pink skin.

"No, I like that one best," said Jasmine. "The black and white splotches are adorable."

"I like them all the best," May declared.

It was Monday afternoon. School was finished for the day, and the three girls were at Corey's house. They were lying on their stomachs, watching a newborn litter of puppies sleeping next to their mother. The mother was a patient of Doc Tock's, and the six puppies had been born at Corey's house the night before.

"I wish I got along with my sisters as well as these puppies get along with one another," May said glumly.

Corey raised an eyebrow as she and Jasmine looked at each other. May was still brooding about her sisters.

"Did they tease you again about ponies?" Corey asked.

May nodded. "And about having their parties in the basement first. But I figured out how to get back at them. You'll see."

"What do you mean?" Jasmine asked.

"I found Dottie's diary," May began. "And I'm sure there are a lot of things in it. I was thinking of reading it out loud to her friends at her first party."

"You wouldn't!" gasped Corey.

"May! Diaries are private," Jasmine chimed in. "You'd be sorry if you did that."

"Don't worry," May promised her. "I won't do anything I'm going to be sorry about."

"Promise?" Corey asked.

May Takes the Lead

"Promise," May said. She meant it, too. She wouldn't be the least bit sorry if she embarrassed Dottie in front of her friends.

Just then two of the puppies woke up and started nuzzling their mother for some milk.

"Aww," said Jasmine.

"You're so lucky that your mom's a vet," May told Corey. "You get to have lots of adorable animals at your house all the time."

"They're not always so adorable," Corey said. "Once we kept a skunk for a week."

"Pee-yew!" said Jasmine.

"Oh, it couldn't spray anything," Corey replied. "Its sprayer had been removed. It was just sort of nasty and nippy. Mom and I didn't know why anyone would want to keep it for a pet. We only had to keep it until it got over its infection. And then there was the time someone brought in a porcupine with pneumonia."

"How did your mom take care of a porcupine with pneumonia?" Jasmine asked.

"Very carefully!" said Corey. The girls laughed. "Most of the time when they're wild animals, Mom takes care of them at CARL instead of here."

The phone rang. Corey answered it.

"Um, yeah, well, uh . . . I think I'd better change phones," she said. Then she turned to Jasmine. "Will you hang this up for me when I pick it up in the kitchen?" she asked. Jasmine said sure. Corey left the room. Jasmine listened at the receiver for a few minutes and then hung up the extension.

"Who was that?" May asked, wondering why Corey would have to go to the kitchen to talk to someone. The Pony Tails were best friends. They never had secrets from one another.

Jasmine seemed a little flustered by the question. "What makes you think *I* know?" she asked.

"Well, you were listening for a while," May told her.

"Oh, right. Well, it was probably a salesman or something," Jasmine mumbled.

That doesn't make any sense at all, May thought.

"Oh, look, the one I like is waking up!" Jasmine said.

May Takes the Lead

May watched as the little puppy stretched, yawned, and wriggled. One of its brothers or sisters—May couldn't tell which—stretched and wriggled and moved so that it was right behind the first puppy. And then a third did the same thing. They looked as if they were lining up to play Follow the Leader or be in a parade.

"Ohhh," May said. The puppies were so cute she forgot all about Corey's strange phone call, at least until Corey came back into the room.

"Who was that?" May asked her friend.

"Um, it was a call," Corey told her, even though May obviously knew that. "It was about CARL," she added quickly. "And the tickets for the show."

"Have they sold any more tickets?" May asked.

"Nope." Corey sighed. "I wish we could think of a way to help."

For a few moments the Pony Tails were silent, each thinking about how they could make the event for CARL a big success.

May stared at the puppies while she thought. There were now four of them lined up, each with its head resting on the next one's back. At first it was hard to think about ponies while she was looking at the puppies, but then she saw it.

"A parade!" she announced.

For a minute Jasmine thought her friend had lost her mind. "No, we're doing a drill exercise for CARL, not a parade," she corrected May.

"I know that!" May told her. "But if we have a parade, everybody will see us and they'll wonder why and we can tell them about the show we're putting on. Parades are fun!"

"Right," Corey said. "But just exactly how—"

"Come on, you guys. Nobody can ignore a parade," May went on, the words tumbling out. "Especially if it's something totally wonderful like a pony parade. We can go all around the town and into the shopping center. Lots of people go there. They'll all notice us and watch. Everyone loves a parade, right?"

May Takes the Lead

"You could be right about—" said Jasmine.

"You bet I am," May interrupted. "And the time to do it is this weekend. Definitely this weekend. Because the show is *next* weekend. Now, we have to do it on Saturday." She stopped talking for a minute to think. "Saturday afternoon, definitely," she said. "That's when most people are shopping."

"Good idea!" said Jasmine.

Then Corey spoke up. "Saturday afternoon isn't a very good idea," she said quickly. "Saturday morning's much better."

"What's the matter with Saturday afternoon?" May asked.

"Didn't you promise Dottie and Ellie that you'd help them finish the basement cleanup on Saturday afternoon because Dottie has some friends coming over?" Corey asked.

"I did?" May asked. "Oh, right, maybe I did." She stared at her friend, confused. "But how did you know? Dottie just told me about that last night."

"Saturday morning's a better time," Corey went on. "Even more people are shopping on Saturday morning than Saturday afternoon."

"They are?" May asked.

"Definitely," Jasmine agreed.

"Then I guess it's Saturday morning—that is, if Max agrees," May said. Max Regnery was the owner of Pine Hollow Stables. That was where the girls had riding lessons and Pony Club meetings.

"Why don't you call him now?" Corey suggested. "You can use the phone in the kitchen."

"Okay." May hurried to the kitchen. She was so excited she could hardly stand it.

The parade would be a smashing success—she just knew it. In fact, the whole day would be wonderful. On Saturday after the parade, Dottie's friends would come over. Then May could reveal all Dottie's juicy secrets!

She punched in the digits for Pine Hollow Stables. "Hello, Max," May began. "I have the most wonderful idea. . . ."

6 A Family Dinner

At dinner that night Ellie told everyone how she'd scored a goal at soccer that afternoon. Then Dottie talked about the new substitute math teacher. She thought he was *really* cute.

May thought this was the most boring dinner table talk in the world. She wondered how Jasmine and Corey could possibly wish they had sisters.

"And how are plans coming for the CARL show?" Mr. Grover asked May.

"Oh, great!" she said enthusiastically. "In fact, something big just came up this afternoon."

"What's that, dear?" Mrs. Grover asked.

"A parade," May announced. Dottie and Ellie seemed about as interested in that as May had been in soccer and the substitute math teacher. "But not just a parade, a *pony* parade!" she went on anyway. "It was my idea. And Max and Mrs. Reg think it's a really good idea."

"What's a pony parade?" her mother asked.

"We're going to have a parade that starts at Pine Hollow and goes all over town," May began. "It will be a way of letting everybody know about the show for CARL. We'll make some banners and pass out flyers to everybody. We're going to do it on Saturday," she added.

"Not Saturday *afternoon?*" said Dottie. She looked worried.

"It's okay," May said. "I'll be there to help out in the basement. I didn't forget about your party."

"Good," said Dottie. "Because I've got about twenty-five people coming over Saturday night. I want the place to be really clean."

May Takes the Lead

"I hope you won't be too tired to work after your little parade," Ellie said.

"If you're going to be marching all over town—" Dottie began.

May felt her face turning bright red. Before she could say anything herself, Mr. Grover cut Dottie off. "That's enough!" he said sharply. Dottie looked at him and stopped talking. "May, that sounds like a wonderful idea," he told her. "It's very creative. You're sure to make a lot of people curious about the show. Nice thinking."

"Thanks, Dad." May smirked at her sisters. She couldn't help it. At least *one* member of the family understood how important ponies were.

May ate the rest of her meal in silence. As soon as she could, she excused herself. "I've got homework to do," she announced.

She ran up the stairs and along the hall and into her room. She closed the door behind her.

"Dottie deserves this," she whispered to herself. She still hadn't thought of a way to get back at Ellie, so for now she'd concentrate on Dottie.

Pony Tails

May reached under her bed and took the diary out of the box. Her thumb went to the latch and flicked at the button that should open it. The latch didn't move.

"Locked," May concluded.

What did you expect? she asked herself. It's a diary!

May looked around her room. A paper clip might do the job. Maybe she had one in her desk drawer. But that place was such a mess, she'd never find anything as small as a paper clip in it.

Tomorrow, then. She'd find a paper clip tomorrow and she would try to pick the lock.

For now she had some more math homework to do. She rewrapped the diary and put it back in its hiding place. Then she went to her desk where her math workbook was waiting for her attention. Her assignment sheet was attached to it with a paper clip.

May glanced back at her bed, thinking of the diary in the box underneath it. She could . . .

No, I'll do it tomorrow, she told herself.

7 Taking Charge

At pony class on Wednesday, Max had all the riders line up their ponies in front of him. Everybody knew that meant there was going to be an announcement. There was a buzz of excitement.

"Now, before we begin class," he started, "the Pony Tails have something to tell you about. May?"

May wasn't expecting this. She wasn't sure what she would say. She was sure Corey would say it better.

"Corey, you tell them," May said. Corey did. She told all about the plans for the pony parade. Corey explained that they were going to meet at Pine Hollow at nine-thirty on Saturday morning and that the parade would begin at ten. The riders' faces glowed with excitement.

"What are we supposed to wear?" Jackie Rogers asked.

"Your best riding clothes," Max answered. "We want everybody to know how good we really are."

"So they'll all want to watch us do the really hard things at the demonstration!" said Amie Connor.

"This is a *great* idea," said Jessica Adler.

"Definitely," Jackie added.

"I'm telling my mother to be sure to do her shopping on Saturday morning," said Josh Jackson. "I don't want her to miss this!"

"It *is* a good idea," Max agreed. "But it's going to take a lot of organization. I need one person who will help my mother and me coordinate everything. Do I have a volunteer?"

There was a long silence. Max looked at all the riders. All the riders looked at each other. May looked at Corey. Corey shook

May Takes the Lead

her head ever so slightly. May looked at Jasmine. Jasmine shook her head hard.

"We can't do this without help," Max said.

"What about Lisa Atwood?" Jackie asked.

"No, this is a pony parade," May reminded her. "It's just for the younger riders on ponies."

"Everybody wants to ride in the parade, but nobody wants to work on it?" Max looked annoyed.

"Come on, guys," May said. "Somebody's got to be in charge!"

"What about *you?*" Amie asked.

"Me?" May said.

"Yes, you," said Corey.

"But I'm not organized," said May.

"It *was* your idea," Max reminded her.

"But—" May protested.

"Hey, May, you're going to do a wonderful job!" said Jasmine. "You know exactly what we need to do to make it a success. Nobody would do it better."

"I agree. It's decided then, May, and thank you for volunteering," said Max.

"But—"

"May, while we warm up our ponies, why don't you go in and talk with Mrs. Reg to see what needs to be done?" Max suggested. "Jasmine, you can walk May's pony on a lead line, okay?"

"Sure, Max," Jasmine said.

"And then, at the end of class, we will have a parade practice," Max went on.

May could hardly believe what had happened. She had one little idea, and the next thing she knew, somebody had put her in charge! She didn't want to be in charge. She just wanted to ride in a parade. She had too many other things to think about to be in charge of a parade. She had schoolwork, the drill event for CARL, basement cleaning, plus revenge on her sisters. Could she really add a whole parade on top?

She looked around at the other riders, hoping to find some help. Maybe someone would say they actually thought they could do a better job than May. It wouldn't be hard. May thought *anyone* could do a better job than she could. She was good at ideas. She wasn't good at organization.

"May, give your reins to Jasmine," Max said.

That was it. Max had decided. May was in charge. She sighed and dismounted. She handed the reins to Jasmine and walked into Mrs. Reg's office.

Outside, class was beginning. Inside, it was just May and Mrs. Reg.

"Now, sit down and let's get started," said Mrs. Reg.

May sat down. They got started.

It turned out that Mrs. Reg had already made a long list of things that needed to be done. One person needed to be the equipment manager. That person would be in charge of making sure that everybody was there and properly dressed. Another person would work with Mrs. Reg to be sure everybody had flyers to hand out to people watching the parade. And then they would need some people at the shopping center who could sell tickets to the drill team event. Obviously that would be another person who wasn't riding in the parade. Mrs. Reg had already called the chief of police to be sure they had permission for their parade.

"That was easy," Mrs. Reg said. "He rides here at Pine Hollow on his day off."

Mrs. Reg told May that somebody ought to call the managers of the stores at the shopping center to be sure they knew about the parade so they could tell their customers.

"And most important, we have to have one person in charge of the actual pony parade—the leader," said Mrs. Reg.

"Shouldn't that be Max?" May asked.

"He's too big to ride a pony," Mrs. Reg said. "It should be one of the young riders."

"Oh," said May.

"Now, your main job will be finding people to do all these jobs," said Mrs. Reg.

"Nobody wanted *this* job," May wailed. "How will I find people to do other jobs?"

"If you want the pony parade to be a success, you'll find them," said Mrs. Reg.

She gave May a list of the jobs she had to fill. Before May could ask one more

May Takes the Lead

question, Mrs. Reg picked up her pen and started writing. May knew she was being dismissed.

In class, the riders were having one final run-through of the drill exercise they would perform at the show. May hurried to catch up. For the next half hour, she was working too hard to think about the work she'd have to do when they stopped riding.

Then it was time for a break—a break for everybody but May.

"Corey, can you be the equipment manager?" May asked. Corey was the most organized person she knew, and this job required a lot of organization.

"I'm sorry, May." Corey shook her head. "I can't do that. I've got too much to do for the drill exercise already. Remember, I'm in the main part of the show, but I'm also in the small group."

May remembered. Max had picked a small group of riders to perform extra skills in the show. Corey was very busy with that.

"Jasmine?" May pleaded.

"No way," Jasmine said. "I've got a big school project coming up and I'm going to have to work on it every spare second over the weekend. . . ."

May hadn't known about Jasmine's school project. Projects were important. No wonder Jasmine couldn't help her.

"Erin, could you—?" Erin Mosley wasn't May's favorite rider at the stable, but May was getting desperate.

"Are you going to ask me to help with the pony parade?" Erin snapped.

May nodded.

Erin tossed her long blond hair. "I'll help you plan the lineup—I think we should go by height."

It didn't surprise May that Erin wanted to go by height. Erin's pony was very small. That would put her in the lead.

"No thanks," May said.

She turned to find someone else.

"Josh, would you like to call all the stores at the shopping center?" she asked.

"You mean, like on the telephone?" Josh asked. May remembered that Josh was very shy. Asking him to make phone calls probably wasn't a good idea.

May Takes the Lead

"Actually, how would you like to be in charge of being sure everybody has flyers to hand out?" May asked.

"Me?" Josh asked.

"Yes, you," May said.

"Wow," he said.

May put a check mark by that item on her list. It was the easiest job by far, but it was filled. If Jasmine and Corey were too busy to be equipment manager, maybe they could give her a hand by calling some of the stores. They weren't shy about making phone calls.

May looked around for her friends. Jasmine was talking with Jackie. May saw Jasmine hand a piece of paper to Jackie. As soon as May called Jasmine's name, Jackie stuffed the paper in her pocket. May thought that was odd, but sometimes Jackie acted odd.

She turned to look for Corey. Corey was whispering something to Amie. Amie giggled. May thought Amie giggled too much. She decided not to ask Corey anything. Just as she started to turn away, Corey handed Amie an envelope. Amie stuck it in her pocket right away.

"All right, everybody. Let's mount up again," Max announced, looking up at the cloudy sky. "I want to get in some practice time for the pony parade before it rains. Are you ready, May?"

"Yes," May mumbled. As she climbed into the saddle, she couldn't help feeling a little annoyed. Nobody wanted to help her with the pony parade. Everybody was too busy with school projects, drill team work, and giggling to give her a hand.

There was only one answer, then. May would take charge. Maybe she wasn't the most organized person in the world, but she could do this. And since nobody else wanted to do any of the hard things, then nobody else was going to do the most fun thing—take the lead in the parade.

"Okay, riders," May shouted when everyone had mounted. "Follow me."

A light rain started to fall as May rode toward some poles Max had set up in the schooling ring.

Slowly the other riders fell in line.

8 Something in the Air

"But, Mr. Michaels, I just want to tell you that there will be a parade on Sat—A parade," May said again. "Actually, a pony parade. No, they're not really young horses, they're small hor— But that's not what's imp—"

May glared at the telephone, wishing she could finish a sentence. The man who owned the shoe shop at the shopping center was having a lot of trouble understanding why there was going to be a pony parade.

"We're raising money for—No, not ponies . . . No, there's no charge for the pony parade, but we'll be selling—Okay, see you then, Mr. Michaels." She hung up. Making phone calls to strangers could be hard.

The good news was that that was the last call. She put a check mark by "Call shopkeepers" on Mrs. Reg's list.

May was sitting at the desk in her mother's office. She felt very important to be at a desk with a telephone. She'd finished one job and she was ready for another. She looked back at Mrs. Reg's list.

Next came figuring out a parade order. A parade could look nice if it went short to tall, as Erin had suggested. But May thought it made more sense to have an experienced rider behind each of the novices, as they called the newest riders. She picked up a pencil and two clean sheets of paper. On the first she wrote the name of every rider in her pony class. Then she noted whether each was an experienced rider or a novice. On the second sheet she made an order, alternating them. Naturally, she also wanted to have her two best friends as close to her as possible.

May Takes the Lead

"First Jasmine, then Jackie, then, um . . ." She wrote the names down.

The phone rang.

"I'll get it!" Dottie yelled from the living room.

May ignored the phone and Dottie. If she put Jasmine first and then Jackie, there might be a problem, because Jackie liked to ride Ha'penny and Ha'penny didn't like Jasmine's pony, Outlaw. He might try to nip at him. That wouldn't be good for the pony parade.

Maybe Nickel should come behind Jasmine. But Josh would probably ride Nickel, and he was just about the newest rider there. It would be better to have Josh in the middle of the parade. But then, if she put—

The phone rang again. May glared at it.

"I'll get it!" Ellie said.

May tried to remember where she was in planning the parade. Right, who would come after Outlaw. Peso? If she put Peso next, then she couldn't put Corey behind Peso because Peso and Corey's pony, Sam, didn't like each other. So, it should be—

RRRRrrringggg!

"I'll get it!" Dottie said.

What's going on here? May asked herself. She couldn't concentrate with the phone ringing like this. Dottie and Ellie always liked to answer the phone, but they didn't usually pounce on it as fast as they were doing today. May decided that they probably each had a new boyfriend. And that meant Dottie's new boyfriend would probably be here on Saturday. And after May read Dottie's diary, they'd never see him again! And Dottie would never get another phone call and the whole house would be quiet!

She turned back to the order of the parade. Maybe it would work better if she had Corey and Sam right behind her, then she could put—

"May, phone call," Dottie said. "It's Corey."

May put down her pencil and picked up the phone.

"How's it coming?" Corey asked.

May told her what she was working on. "It's not easy to concentrate here," she

May Takes the Lead

complained. "The phone keeps ringing off the hook."

"You're getting a lot of calls?" Corey asked.

"No, Ellie and Dottie are," May said.

"Oh," Corey said. "Well, I just wanted to know how you were doing."

"Fine," said May. "See you at the bus tomorrow." They said good night and May got back to work.

If she put Sam and Corey right behind her, then she could put Amie behind . . .

The phone hadn't rung.

The thought came to May as she stared down at the names on the paper in front of her. When Corey called her, the phone hadn't rung. Dottie had answered it and talked for a long time before she yelled that it was Corey for May. What could they have said to each other?

May felt a twinge in the pit of her stomach. Corey hadn't liked the idea that May had the diary. Was it possible she'd told Dottie? May gulped. She had to know.

She put down the pencil and went into

the living room where both her sisters were doing homework.

"Hi, guys," she said.

"Hi, May," they said back.

Neither of them looked as if they wanted to strangle her. That was a good sign. But maybe they were just pretending. She had an idea.

"Could you two do me a favor?" she asked.

"Like what?" Ellie eyed her suspiciously.

"Well, you know about the pony parade on Saturday morning?" May began.

"Sure, we know about it," said Dottie.

"I need someone at the shopping center to sell tickets to the drill team demonstration while the parade is on. Could you do that?"

"Oh, come on, May," Ellie said. "You know there's a lot to do for the party—"

"Not that much," Dottie interrupted. May could have sworn she nudged Ellie. "How much help will you need?"

"About an hour?" May said. "Maybe ten to eleven?"

"Okay," Ellie said. "We'll be there."

"You will?" May said.

"Sure," Dottie said. "Glad to help."

"Thanks," May said. She returned to her mother's office.

Why had Dottie nudged Ellie? she wondered. And why had both her sisters acted so nice to her?

There was only one answer.

Something was up. But what?

9 The Pony Parade

"Riders, forward!" May called. Then she nudged Macaroni and moved ahead herself. She could hear the wonderful clop of fifteen ponies' hooves behind her. The parade had started!

And so far, if she didn't count the fact that two of the riders were wearing jeans instead of proper riding pants, everything was going smoothly. May couldn't believe it. She'd done it and she'd done it right!

"Come on, Macaroni," she told her pony. "All the work is done. Let's have fun!"

May and Mrs. Reg had planned the

parade route carefully. May was to lead the riders along the road through downtown Willow Creek, from the town green to the shopping center. From there they could take the shortcut through the woods back to Pine Hollow.

"Riders, prepare to trot!" May called. She and Macaroni began trotting toward the green. Behind her, fifteen riders started trotting as well. When the path narrowed and there were more cars on the road, May held up her hand, signaling a walk. She reined Macaroni in. He walked. Behind her, fifteen riders and their ponies returned to a walk.

Soon the ponies got closer to the middle of town.

"Hey, look! Ponies!" said a little girl who was playing with dolls in the front yard of her house.

"Wow!" said her friend.

"Come watch us ride and help CARL," Josh said. He reached out and handed the girls one of the flyers Mrs. Reg had made up for them.

"Okay," said the first little girl. Then she

turned to her friend. "Come on, let's call Francesca and tell her."

Francesca, it turned out, lived just down the street. By the time the ponies got to Francesca's house, the girls had also called other friends. At every house along the way, people came out to watch. And every person who came to watch got a flyer telling them about the following week's drill demonstration for the animal shelter.

"CARL? I know about that," said one man. "They do good work. I can help them just by watching you ride?"

"You sure can," said Josh. "Buy a ticket to the show and bring some friends. That will help even more."

May could hardly believe what was happening to Josh. The shy boy wasn't at all shy when he was talking about CARL!

The cry of "Hey, ponies!" followed them everywhere. By the time they got to the center of town, all the firefighters were standing in front of the firehouse and cheering for them. Every one of them got a flyer from Josh or one of the other riders. May thought she'd never sat so tall in the saddle. She was proud of her parade.

While a policeman stopped traffic, the riders crossed the main road to the town green. It was a park and it was full of people this morning. The pony parade was already getting people's attention, but May knew she could do more.

"Prepare to trot!" she called out, raising her hand. She took the riders in a big circle all around the town green at a trot. Then she cut across the circle to make a figure eight. When she'd finished that, she started riding around the trees on the green.

"Hey, this is neat!" said Amie. She was having fun, and so were all the other riders.

"Look, Mom. Horsies!" a little girl said, tugging at her mother's hand.

"Do you like horsies?" the mother asked.

"I *love* horsies!" the little girl said.

Josh gave them a flyer. "Tickets on sale at the shopping center," he told them. "Don't miss the show!"

May Takes the Lead

"Let's go, Mommy!" said the little girl.

It was working, *really* working! May was so happy she punched the air with her fist and yelled "Yahoo!" Behind her fifteen riders punched the air with their fists and yelled "Yahoo!"

That was when May realized they weren't just having a pony parade. They were playing Follow the Leader! May knew how to lead that better than anyone, and so she did.

She brought Macaroni back to a walk. Then she stood up in her stirrups. Behind her, fifteen riders stood up, too, one by one. Then May sat down. They all sat down, one by one.

She swung her right arm in an arc. All the other riders swung their right arms in an arc. She put her left hand on top of her riding helmet. Everybody else did the same.

At first, only a few people on the green were paying attention. But by the time May had the riders turning their ponies in circles, everybody was watching.

"It's a show!" said one man.

"Come see some more!" said Josh. More flyers went out to the people in town.

"Tickets on sale at the shopping center," said Corey.

"Don't miss the big fun!" said Jasmine.

"Pay attention to May," said Jackie. "She's going to do something else wacky."

They did and she did. May took her feet out of her stirrups and stuck them straight out in front of her. Then she brought her feet back and leaned forward into Macaroni's mane.

People started clapping when they saw how well everybody played the game. May didn't want to show people too much, though. She wanted to be sure they knew they would see even better riding at the CARL show.

"Let's take our show on the road!" she said. It was time to ride on to the shopping center. May led the parade through town and over to where it seemed most of the people were spending money on this sunny Saturday morning.

May Takes the Lead

Cheers greeted them when they arrived in front of the supermarket. Another sight that greeted them was Dottie and Ellie at a card table, selling tickets as fast as they could make change.

May marched the parade all around the parking lot of the shopping center. A policeman was directing traffic and keeping cars away from the riders.

May spotted an empty part of the parking lot. "May we go over there, sir?" she asked the policeman.

"Sure," he said. He held traffic so that the line of riders could go to the open space.

At the town green May had only worked up an appetite for Follow the Leader. She was going to put on another show here!

As soon as May began the game, people came over to watch. May did everything she'd done before. People clapped. She looked behind her to be sure everybody was following. The riders all looked behind, too. People laughed. May clapped her hand over her mouth to stifle a giggle. All the other riders did the same. So did the audience. May stood up, sat down, leaned back, leaned forward. All the riders followed her and everybody in the audience did, too! It was the biggest game of Follow the Leader that had ever been, and May was in the lead.

She held up her hand to signal a stop. Behind her all the riders came to an orderly halt. May took off her hat and bowed to the audience. So did all the other riders. She just had one more thing she wanted to lead everybody to do.

"My next move is to go over to that table there and buy tickets for the drill team demonstration to raise money for CARL. Will you all follow me and do the same thing there, too?"

Then her audience laughed.

"You don't have to go first on that one," a man in the audience said. "This time I'll be the leader."

And he was. He went right over to the table and bought tickets for the show. Almost everybody else followed him.

They were selling a ton of tickets! May's

pony parade was a bigger success than anyone could have imagined.

May beamed with pride. Behind her, fifteen other riders beamed with pride, too.

Then it was time to go home. May led the way.

10 Back to the Basement

"May, you were great!"

"Wonderful!"

"I never had so much fun on my pony!"

"Wow, did you see all those people buying tickets?"

"Nice job, May."

The compliments still rang in May's ears. It was a wonderful feeling to have done something hard and done it right. At first she'd been a little mad about having to take charge. But being in the lead had been fun—especially since the whole thing had worked out so well.

She was still feeling a glow of happiness

when she unloaded Macaroni from the van and took him into his stall.

"I never could have done it without you," she said. "And now you deserve the biggest, best grooming in the whole wide world."

Macaroni looked at her. He was waiting for his grooming.

May hated to disappoint him. "I'm sorry, good boy," she said. "But I have to be in the basement to help Ellie and Dottie in exactly five minutes. They'll be so mad at me if I don't show up."

Macaroni blinked his huge brown eyes. For the first time in a week, May didn't feel furious at her sisters. After all, they'd been a big help to her today.

"But they still deserve revenge, Macaroni," she told her pony. "They're making me clean the basement so Dottie can have her stupid party first. Just wait till tonight when Dottie's friends come over. I'll show them. . . ."

The back door to her house slammed. A second later Jasmine and Corey dashed into the stable. May was surprised that they'd finished grooming their ponies so quickly. She was even more surprised that they'd come from her house instead of from across the lawn.

"Wasn't that parade wonderful?" Jasmine asked.

"Dottie said they sold over a hundred tickets. Wait till Mom hears that!" said Corey.

Jasmine patted Macaroni. "Good boy," she said. "You deserve a nice grooming."

"I know he does, but I've got to get back to cleaning the basement," said May.

"You can't walk out on Macaroni now!" Corey said. "He did such a great job."

"I know, but—" May began.

"Come on, May. That's not fair to him," said Jasmine.

May tried again. "But I promised my sisters—"

"Give me a break," Corey said. "All week you've been talking about getting revenge on them; now you're worried about breaking a promise?"

May shook her head. "That's not it. . . ." She didn't finish. She didn't know how to tell her friends the real reason she wanted to go inside and help Dottie and Ellie. The other Pony Tails didn't have sisters. They wouldn't understand that it was part of her plan to get back at Dottie that night.

"Come on, May. We'll help you groom Macaroni," Jasmine offered.

"Okay." May gave in finally. "But if the phone rings . . ."

"Don't worry. We're the Pony Tails. We can groom a pony in . . . two shakes of a pony's tail!" said Corey.

Eagerly Corey and Jasmine pitched in to help. May had never seen them so enthusiastic.

"Shampoo!" said Jasmine.

"Cream rinse!" said Corey.

May was helpless to stop Jasmine and Corey from doing the best grooming any pony had ever seen. It was also the clumsiest grooming May had ever seen.

First, Jasmine put the rinse on before Corey used the shampoo.

"Okay, we'll start from the beginning," said Corey. They washed off the rinse and put the shampoo on.

May Takes the Lead

"Why don't you clean his tack while we do this?" Jasmine suggested to May.

"I'll get the saddle soap for you," said Corey. She went to the tack room, but came back with oil instead of saddle soap. "Whoops," said Corey. "I'll take it back." She took it back and returned with the saddle soap—ten minutes later.

"It was sort of hidden," Corey explained.

May knew that wasn't true. The saddle soap was always kept handy on the bottom shelf—the easiest thing to find in the whole tack room.

What was the matter with her friends?

When Jasmine went to the house for a bucket of water, May started to feel worried. There was a perfectly good hose right there in the barn.

"Are you two okay?" May asked Corey.

"Well, we're a little tired from the parade and all," Corey answered.

May thought they were more than a little tired. And she became convinced of it when they finally finished grooming Macaroni. That's when they let him loose in the paddock.

"No, don't!" May called out. But it was too late. The first thing Macaroni did when he got into the paddock was the first thing he *always* did when he got into the paddock. He lay down on the ground, rolled over, and wriggled happily. Every bit of the work they'd done grooming him was now ruined by muddy dirt!

"I guess we'll just have to start all over again," Corey said matter-of-factly.

May was so frustrated, she wanted to scream. "I can groom Macaroni later," she said firmly. "Now I've got to get to the basement."

"No," said Jasmine. "You don't."

"Why not?" May asked.

Jasmine stammered. Corey answered for her. "Because Ellie and Dottie aren't there yet."

"How do you know that?" May asked.

"We came through your house, remember?" Jasmine reminded her.

"And why did you come through my house?" May asked.

"To see if Ellie and Dottie were working yet," said Corey.

Pony Tails

May was beginning to think that her friends weren't exactly pony crazy, but just *plain* crazy. Jasmine started brushing at the dirt on Macaroni's coat. May started to remind her that it could wait when Corey asked May a question.

"Have you considered changing Macaroni's feed during the cooler months of the year?" she asked. "I read something in *Horseplay* about a special blend. Want to try it now? Hey, where's your coffee can? That's a good way to measure grains."

But May couldn't take any more. "No," she said. "I do not want to change Macaroni's grains for the season. And *no,* I do not want to give Macaroni another shampoo. And since you are probably about to ask, I don't want to try a new hunt clip for his coat, or spend the next four hours cleaning his teeth or looking in his ears for ticks."

Corey and Jasmine stared at her as she continued.

"I want to go into the basement and help my sisters before they start screaming at me. So you can stay here, shampoo, mix grains, or try a new hunt clip. I'm going inside!"

May was so annoyed with her friends that she threw down the towel she was holding. Then she marched back toward the house.

Without another look backward, May stormed into the kitchen, pulled open the basement door, flicked on the staircase light, and went down into the darkness. In spite of all the "help" she'd gotten from Corey and Jasmine, she was still getting to the job before her sisters. That was a relief.

When she got to the bottom step, she reached for the next light switch and flipped it on.

"Surprise!"

May gasped. Standing in a big circle all around her were twenty-five of her friends and family members. Everybody had a balloon that said "Happy Birthday, May!" The place was decorated with crepe paper twists.

"But it's—" May began.

May Takes the Lead

Ellie and Dottie came out of the crowd and gave May hugs.

"We know it's not your birthday yet. Not for another couple of days, but if we'd waited until then, it wouldn't have been a surprise, would it?" Ellie asked.

May shook her head. She opened her mouth, but no words came out. She'd never been so surprised in her whole life.

Jasmine and Corey were standing behind her, huge grins on their faces.

"Now it's my turn to be surprised," said Jasmine. "For once in her life, May Grover has nothing to say!"

11 A Red-Letter Day

"I never had more fun at a birthday party," May said to Jasmine and Corey after the last guest had left.

"So you're not still mad at us for grooming Macaroni?" Corey asked.

May laughed. Corey and Jasmine did too.

"I guess not," May told Corey. "So, you guys have been sneaking around all week, trying to fool me about the party?"

"Yup," said Jasmine, looking proud. "So have your sisters. Dottie pretended she was having a party tonight. Actually, Dottie's party isn't until next week!"

May Takes the Lead

"What about the phone call Corey got that day at her house?" she asked Jasmine.

"It was Ellie," Jasmine confessed. "I didn't think you believed the part about the salesman."

"I didn't," May admitted. "But I forgot about it." She remembered something else. "I wondered how you two knew I'd promised to clean the basement this afternoon. Now I know. And is this why you two kept saying all those nice things about my sisters?"

"Well, sure. The whole time you were talking about revenge, they were planning a party for you," Corey said. "We thought that was pretty nice."

May nodded.

The girls giggled as they told all the tricks they'd used to fool May. Every one of them had worked, too. Now the last gift had been opened, the last piece of cake had been eaten, the last game had been played.

The Pony Tails couldn't agree on the most fun part of the party.

Pony Tails

"I liked Pin the Tail on Macaroni best," said May. Her friends had drawn a big picture of Macaroni without his tail. Jackie had managed to pin the tail closest, though May thought she might have peeked through the blindfold.

"You just say that because you put the tail on his nose!" Corey teased.

May laughed. "It showed me what he would look like with a beard."

"My favorite part was making a mural," said Jasmine. Mrs. Grover had covered one wall with huge sheets of paper and let everybody draw pictures.

"Of course that was your favorite," said Corey. "You're very good at art."

"So are you," said Jasmine. "I really loved the elephant you drew."

"It was supposed to be a pony!" said Corey.

May smiled happily, listening to her friends. They'd had as good a time as she had. It *had* been a wonderful party for everyone.

Everybody agreed that the basement room in the Grovers' house was a great place to have parties. They all said they wanted to come to the next one—even her sisters.

That had been the biggest surprise of all. While May and her mother had cut the cake, Dottie and Ellie had made a sort of speech about May.

"Even though she's our sister, we still think she's pretty special, and that's why we wanted you to come to this party for her," Ellie had said.

"But we didn't know how special she was until we saw her in action this morning. That pony parade was great!" said Dottie.

"Great enough to get you to try riding again?" May teased.

"Maybe not *that* great," Ellie said. "But you can bet Dottie and I will be at the drill demonstration."

"Along with a zillion other people," Dottie said. "We sold more than one hundred tickets just this morning. And it was all because of our sister—oh, and some of the rest of you who followed her lead!"

Inside and outside, May was glowing with pride. Her sisters could be a pain, that was sure, but they cared enough to throw a birthday party for her. They cared enough to help with the pony parade, and they cared enough to tell everyone about something she'd done. Her friends had been right all along. She was lucky to have them.

"I think it's time for me to go home," Jasmine said, suddenly standing up. Just then, the phone rang. May answered it. It was a call from Jasmine's mother, telling her to come home for dinner.

"How does she do that?" Corey asked May. "How does she always know when it's time to go home?"

"Beats me." May shrugged.

"I just *know*," Jasmine explained.

"Well, then it must be time for me to go, too," Corey said. May hugged both of her best friends and thanked them for being sneaky and awful.

After the door closed behind them, she realized that it was time to thank her sisters for being sneaky and awful, too.

12 Sisters

May carried her birthday presents back up to her room and piled them on her bed. She'd gotten three horse and pony books, four posters of ponies, a pair of riding gloves from Ellie, a new bridle from her parents, a lead rope from Jasmine, and a halter from Corey. Everybody knew she loved ponies! There were other gifts as well. The pile on her bed made May remember how much her friends and her sisters cared about her.

Her sisters. May felt a twinge. There was something she had to do. She'd seen Ellie downstairs and thanked her and hugged her for the gloves and the party. Now she had to thank Dottie. That might be harder.

She pulled the storage box out from under her bed. She unfolded the sweatshirt. There was Dottie's diary. May was relieved she'd never opened it, but she was ashamed that she'd even *thought* of reading it.

May sat on the edge of her bed, looking at the diary. What could she do now? She could leave it in the box under her bed. She could put it back in the carton in the basement. She could put it somewhere in Dottie's room. She could even throw it away. Dottie would never know.

But May would. May would know and she wouldn't feel right about it. She knew then what she had to do. She had to return it to Dottie. She had to tell.

She rewrapped the book in her sweatshirt. Dottie's room was across the hall from hers. The door was closed. May knocked.

"Come in," said Dottie.

May went in.

May Takes the Lead

"Dottie, that was the best birthday party anybody ever had," she said.

Dottie smiled proudly. "I know, you already told me and Ellie that about a million times. I just feel bad that I was so busy with all the plans I never got around to getting you a present."

"I don't need any more presents," May said. "Actually I don't deserve any more presents."

"What's the matter, May?" Dottie asked. "That doesn't sound like you."

May unwrapped the diary. "I—"

"Oh, you found that," said Dottie. "I've been looking for it for months! Where was it?"

"It was in the basement," May said. She wanted to blurt it all out at once, but she was so upset that it started coming out in little pieces. "I found it when we were cleaning up. I never knew you had a diary. I've always thought diaries were really great, but I never had one, and I—"

"Would you like one?" Dottie asked.

"Me?" May asked.

"Is there someone else here?" Dottie teased.

May was flustered. "But I didn't . . ." She handed the diary to Dottie. Dottie took it and rubbed her hand gently over the smooth leather cover.

"It's a beauty, isn't it?" she asked. May agreed that it certainly was beautiful. "Uncle Jared gave it to me for Christmas two years ago. I always thought it was too beautiful to ruin with my messy handwriting. Isn't that silly?"

The words sank in. "You mean you never wrote in it?" May said.

"No, didn't you know?" Dottie asked.

"I didn't look," May stammered. "It's locked."

"Oh, the key's right here," said Dottie. She held the book up and squeezed it from side to side to flex the pages. A little key dropped out onto the floor. Dottie picked it up, stuck it in the lock, and turned it. The lock snapped open.

"I never even wrote my name in it," Dottie said. "I always wanted to be the kind of person who could keep a diary, but I'm not. You need to be organized and orderly to do that." She grinned. "You know, like the kind of person who can organize a whole parade in four days."

"Me?" May asked. "You think I could keep a diary?"

"Sure," said Dottie. "You're always doing interesting things that you could write about."

May couldn't believe her sister was talking about her that way. But Dottie was right. She *did* do interesting things. She did them with her friends and with her pony. She could write about Macaroni and everything she learned at riding class and Horse Wise. She could write about things that happened at school or with Pony Tails. Maybe she should take some of the birthday money her parents gave her and buy a diary for herself.

"Here, May. You take this," said Dottie, holding out the diary.

"Oh, no," May stammered. "I . . ."

"Don't be silly. I'll never use it," Dottie said. "You will. I owe you a birthday pres-

ent anyway. And this one will really mean something to you."

May blinked. She took the diary. It would mean something to her. It would mean more than Dottie would ever know. More than May would ever have to tell her.

"Thank you again," she said.

Dottie gave her a hug.

"You're welcome, little sister," she said. "Now go on, get out of my room. I'm expecting a telephone call from Richard and I don't want you to hear a word of it!"

"I promise I won't listen," May said, and she meant it.

13 A Good Grooming

The next morning, bright and early, the Pony Tails met in May's stable to give their ponies a good grooming—a *real* grooming.

"This time we won't let them roll around in the paddock afterward!" May said.

Jasmine and Corey laughed and agreed that that was a good idea. Outlaw looked at Sam and then they both looked at Macaroni.

"I think they're telling each other that we're taking all the fun out!" said May.

"Well, they can roll as much as they want after the drill demonstration next week," said Corey. "For now, they have to stay clean."

The girls got to work with their currycombs. One of the nice things about working on their ponies together was that they could talk as they worked.

"Can I say thank you one more time?" May asked.

"No!" Corey and Jasmine said together. "We had as much fun at the party as you did. Stop thanking us."

"All right," May agreed. "It's just that—"

"May!" Corey and Jasmine shouted at once.

"Jake," Corey cried.

"Jake," Jasmine echoed. Then the two girls did a high five and a low five and shouted "Jake" again. That was what the Pony Tails always did when they said the same thing at the same time.

"Well, the pony parade really helped CARL," said Jasmine as she started brushing Outlaw again.

"It helped me, too," said May. "It reminded me that doing good things is better than doing bad things."

"Does this mean you're not planning revenge on your sisters anymore?" Corey asked.

May nodded. "I think my sisters and I are finally even."

"What happened?" Jasmine asked.

"I'm not sure I can explain it," May told her. "But I'll write about it in my new diary."

"That's a great idea," Corey told her.

"May's full of great ideas," Jasmine said. "That's why she's the best at Follow the Leader."

"Thank you," May told her friends. Then she turned back to the ponies. She wanted to concentrate on the two things she did best of all: taking care of Macaroni and being part of the Pony Tails.

MAY'S TIPS ON RECOGNIZING HORSE BREEDS

If there's one thing I know about breeds of horses and ponies, it's that there are a lot of them. In fact, there are hundreds!

Horse and pony breeds are usually associated with the part of the world from which they come. In other words, Arabians came from the Arabian peninsula; Shetland ponies originated in the Shetland Islands near Scotland; Pasos are from Peru in South America; Fjords are from Scandinavia; and so on. Today horses and ponies can be moved all over the world by vans, boats, and airplanes. It's not unusual to see an Icelandic pony in North America. Before they were transported by humans, horses and ponies pretty much stayed put.

Generally horses and ponies fall into

three groups that mostly have to do with their sizes: draft horses, riding horses, and ponies. Draft horses are very big and very strong. They can be used to pull heavy loads on wagons. Some people call them workhorses. The best-known breeds of draft horses are the Clydesdales, Shires, and Percherons. Clydesdales and Shires came from the British Isles. Percherons came from France. Each of these three kinds of horses are about seventeen hands high. That means they are five feet eight inches tall at their withers! They also have very thick, strong bodies and legs.

There are many breeds of riding horses, but when some people think of riding horses, they think of Thoroughbreds. Most racetrack horses are Thoroughbreds. They are very fast. They can be as tall as draft horses, but they are much sleeker. They are also very beautiful. Thoroughbreds were first bred in England.

Another familiar breed of riding horse is the Arabian. This horse was originally bred to be able to survive in the desert.

May Takes the Lead

Arabians are strong, fast, and have a lot of endurance, and I guess they can go for a long time without water. A lot of people think they are the prettiest breed of horse. Their faces are very delicate-looking.

In the United States, we have a couple of our own breeds. There is the Morgan, which has a broad chest and back and is very strong. All Morgans are descended from a horse that was once owned by a man named Justin Morgan.

Another American breed is the Quarter Horse. This horse was originally ridden by cowboys. Quarter Horses are very fast and smart. They really help the cowboys who are trying to round up stray cattle. They are called Quarter Horses because they run fast for short distances. When they race, they run for a quarter of a mile. I measured it once; I can run a quarter of a mile in about three minutes. The fastest Quarter Horses can run that distance in twenty seconds!

Saddlebreds, or American Saddle horses, are elegant, high-stepping horses from the United States. This breed came from plantations in the South. These horses are comfortable to ride and beautiful to watch because they move so smoothly.

Some breeds are identified by their colors. These include pintos, palominos, and Appaloosas. Pintos have large splotches of white and either brown or black on them. Palominos are a golden color with a silvery mane. Appaloosas are gray or white with small dark spots, especially on their rears.

There are as many breeds of ponies as there are of draft and riding horses—maybe more. When most people think of ponies, they think of Shetlands because they are so common for young beginning riders. Shetlands are small. The tallest is only 10.2 hands—that's just 3 feet 6 inches. They can be headstrong and stubborn.

Jasmine's pony, Outlaw, is a Welsh pony. Welsh ponies came from Wales. They are intelligent and spirited. That's true of Outlaw. It takes a lot of intelligence to be as naughty as he is sometimes!

Pony of the Americas is a new breed.

May Takes the Lead

These ponies were first bred in Iowa from a Shetland stallion and an Appaloosa mare. A lot of people like them because they tend to be polite and reliable. Those are important qualities in a pony that kids are going to ride.

One thing I know about horse and pony breeds is that people become real fans of certain ones. One woman I know will ride only Pasos ponies. Another person thinks Saddlebreds are the only horses to ride. So, you're probably wondering what my favorite breed is. That's easy: Macaroni!

About the Author

Bonnie Bryant was born and raised in New York City, and still lives there today. She spends her summers in a house on a lake in Massachusetts.

Ms. Bryant began writing about girls and horses when she started The Saddle Club in 1987. So far there are more than sixty books in that series. Much as she likes telling the stories about Stevie, Carole, and Lisa, she decided that the younger riders at Pine Hollow Stables, especially May Grover, have stories of their own. That's how Pony Tails was born.

Ms. Bryant rides horses when she has time away from her computer, but she doesn't have a horse of her own. She likes to ride different horses, enjoying a variety of riding experiences. She thinks most of her readers are much better riders than she is!

THE SADDLE CLUB™

❏ 15594-6 HORSE CRAZY #1	$3.50/$4.50 Can.	❏ 15938-0 STAR RIDER #19	$3.50/$4.50 Can.
❏ 15611-X HORSE SHY #2	$3.25/$3.99 Can.	❏ 15907-0 SNOW RIDE #20	$3.50/$4.50 Can.
❏ 15626-8 HORSE SENSE #3	$3.50/$4.50 Can.	❏ 15983-6 RACEHORSE #21	$3.50/$4.50 Can.
❏ 15637-3 HORSE POWER #4	$3.50/$4.50 Can.	❏ 15990-9 FOX HUNT #22	$3.50/$4.50 Can.
❏ 15703-5 TRAIL MATES #5	$3.50/$4.50 Can.	❏ 48025-1 HORSE TROUBLE #23	$3.50/$4.50 Can.
❏ 15728-0 DUDE RANCH #6	$3.50/$4.50 Can.	❏ 48067-7 GHOST RIDER #24	$3.50/$4.50 Can.
❏ 15754-X HORSE PLAY #7	$3.25/$3.99 Can.	❏ 48072-3 SHOW HORSE #25	$3.50/$4.50 Can.
❏ 15769-8 HORSE SHOW #8	$3.25/$3.99 Can.	❏ 48073-1 BEACH RIDE #26	$3.50/$4.50 Can.
❏ 15780-9 HOOF BEAT #9	$3.50/$4.50 Can.	❏ 48074-X BRIDLE PATH #27	$3.50/$4.50 Can.
❏ 15790-6 RIDING CAMP #10	$3.50/$4.50 Can.	❏ 48075-8 STABLE MANNERS #28	$3.50/$4.50 Can.
❏ 15805-8 HORSE WISE #11	$3.25/$3.99 Can..	❏ 48076-6 RANCH HANDS #29	$3.50/$4.50 Can.
❏ 15821-X RODEO RIDER #12	$3.50/$4.50 Can.	❏ 48077-4 AUTUMN TRAIL #30	$3.50/$4.50 Can.
❏ 15832-5 STARLIGHT CHRISTMAS #13	$3.50/$4.50 Can.	❏ 48145-2 HAYRIDE #31	$3.50/$4.50 Can.
❏ 15847-3 SEA HORSE #14	$3.50/$4.50 Can.	❏ 48146-0 CHOCOLATE HORSE #32	$3.50/$4.50 Can.
❏ 15862-7 TEAM PLAY #15	$3.50/$4.50 Can.	❏ 48147-9 HIGH HORSE #33	$3.50/$4.50 Can.
❏ 15882-1 HORSE GAMES #16	$3.25/$3.99 Can.	❏ 48148-7 HAY FEVER #34	$3.50/$4.50 Can.
❏ 15937-2 HORSENAPPED #17	$3.50/$4.50 Can.	❏ 48149-5 A SUMMER WITHOUT HORSES Super #1	$3.99/$4.99 Can.
❏ 15928-3 PACK TRIP #18	$3.50/$4.50 Can.